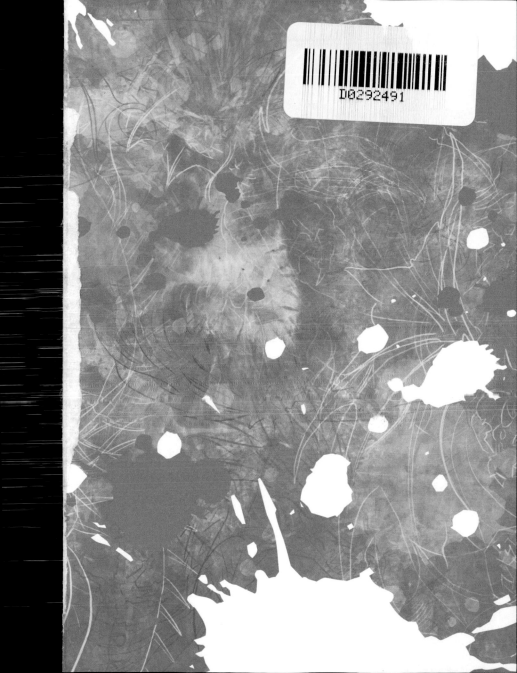

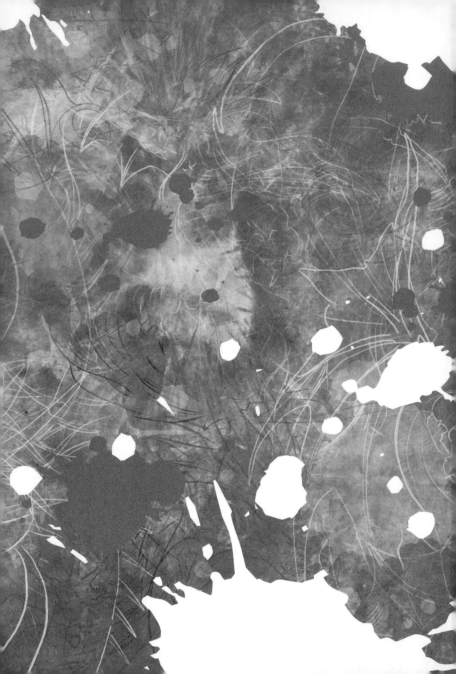

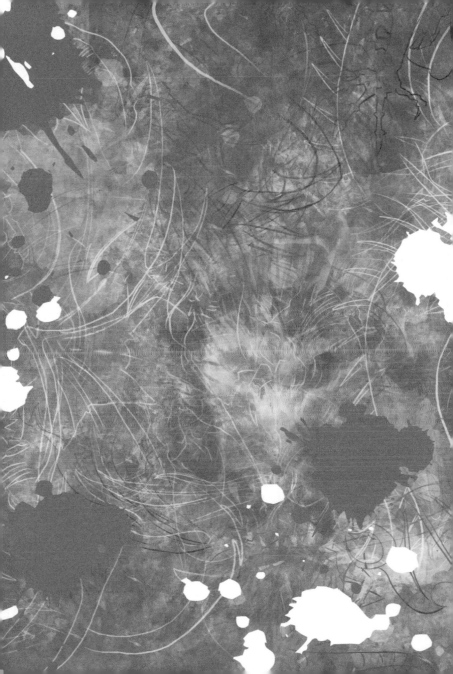

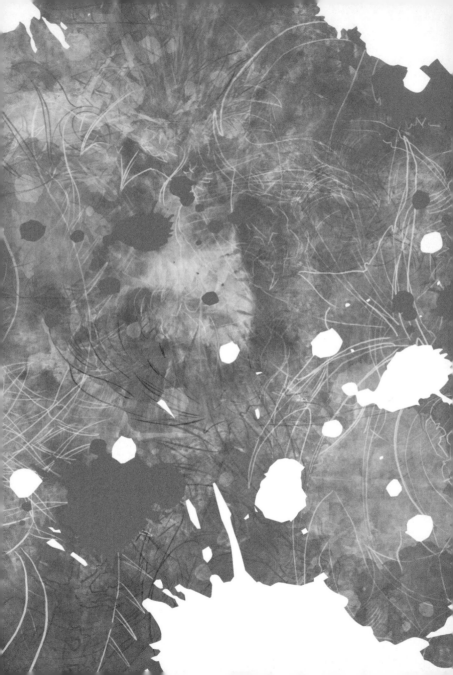

DRAGONBLOOD

DRAGON IN THE DESERT

Michael Dahl

Tou Vue

STONE ARCH BOOKS
www.stonearchbooks.com

Zone Books are published by
Stone Arch Books
A Capstone Imprint
1710 Roe Crest Drive
North Mankato, Minnesota 56003
www.capstonepub.com

Library of Congress Cataloging-in-Publication Data
Dahl, Michael.
    Dragon in the Desert / by Michael Dahl; illustrated
by Tou Vue.
    p. cm. — (Zone Books. Dragonblood)
    ISBN 978-1-4342-1260-3 (library binding)
    ISBN 978-1-4342-2309-8 (softcover)
    [1. Dragons—Fiction. 2. Mongolia—Fiction.] I. Vue, Tou,
1974– ill. II. Title.
PZ7.D15134Dr 2009
[Fic]—dc22   2008031280

Summary: Two teenage friends hike into the deserts
of Mongolia. Their destination: the Hills of the Seven
Dragons. But they are not alone. A third figure walks
through the desert, following their footprints.

Creative Director: Heather Kindseth
Graphic Designer: Brann Garvey

Printed in the United States of America in North Mankato, Minnesota.
022017
010277R

TABLE OF CONTENTS

Introduction

A new Age of Dragons is about to begin. The **powerful** creatures will return to rule the **world** once more, but this time will be **different**. This time, they will have allies. Who will **help** them? Around the world, some young humans are making a strange **discovery**. They are learning that they were born with **dragon blood** – blood that gives them **amazing powers**.

CHAPTER 1

Stranger on a Train

A train chugged across the
vast Mongolian desert.

Shen and Kong stared out the
windows of the train.

They had been friends for years,
since the first day of school.

"Look," said Shen. He pointed
out the window.

A row of brown hills appeared
in the distance.

*"The Hills of the Seven
Dragons,"* whispered Kong.

Kong looked worried. "You don't have to come with me," he said.

"I am your friend," said Shen. "I won't leave now. We've already come this far."

A man was sitting at the other end of the train car.

Carefully, he listened to everything the two friends said to each other.

CHAPTER 2

The Seven Dragons

The train **stopped** at an empty station.

The two friends walked off the train platform.

Behind them, the stranger also got off the train.

Hours later, Shen and Kong walked in the shadow of the brown hills.

Kong pulled a map out of his backpack.

"The cave should be around here," he said.

Suddenly, Kong cried out. **"Ow!"** he yelled.

"What's wrong?" asked Shen.

Kong rubbed his shoulder. "It's my **birthmark** again," he said. "It's **burning.**"

"Look over there," said Shen.

Halfway up a hill was the mouth of a cave.

It was hidden in shadow.

If Kong hadn't stopped to rub his shoulder, the two boys would have missed it.

CHAPTER 3
The Cave

The hot desert *sun* beat down on the hills.

Kong pulled off his shirt.

Shen could see the birthmark on his friend's shoulder.

The mark reminded him of a dragon.

"How long do you have to stay inside the cave?" asked Shen.

"Until *sunrise*," said Kong. "That is what my grandfather told me to do."

"He told me that if I do this, I will become **powerful**," added Kong.

Kong's green eyes were full of determination.

Kong took his backpack and climbed up to the cave.

Shen waved as his friend **disappeared** inside the dark opening.

CHAPTER 4
Aliens

Shen sat and waited.

He thought about Kong's grandfather.

Kong's grandfather was a famous scientist and *astronomer*.

He believed that <u>aliens</u> had visited Earth thousands of years ago.

The aliens looked like reptiles, he claimed. Or like dragons.

Many people thought Kong's grandfather was crazy.

Shen didn't know what to think.

He knew that Kong was doing this strange task to please his grandfather. And he knew that Kong needed his help.

Shen also wondered why the hills were called the **Seven Dragons.**

There were only six hills.

Suddenly, the six hills began to **shake.**

CHAPTER 5
The Seventh Dragon

A burst of flame shot from the cave.

"Kong!" shouted Shen. "Where are you?"

A creature crawled out of the cave. It flapped its mighty wings.

Then it looked down at Shen.

Shen stared at the dragon's green eyes.

A warm *breeze* brushed against his skin.

He felt calm.

The stranger from the train ran out of the shadows.

"You must not return!" he shouted.

He aimed an evil-looking weapon at the **dragon.**

The dragon shot **flames** toward the man.

The fire melted the sand around the man's feet.

The sand turned into hard glass.

The man dropped his weapon. He could not move.

The dragon **roared** and disappeared into the sky.

Shen escaped into the

darkness.

He ran toward the lonely train
station.

Shen knew that Kong no longer
needed his help.

He also knew that he would
never see his friend again.

Of Dragons and Near-Dragons

In ancient and modern-day China, dragons are an important part of popular culture. Dragons are symbols of male strength, energy, and royalty.

If you find dragons in Chinese paintings and sculptures, most of them have 117 scales. They also have five toes on each foot.

Today in China, if someone wishes their son will "be a dragon," it means they hope that he will become successful and happy.

Ancient Chinese emperors believed that they were descended from dragons. They wore dragon robes, sat on dragon thrones, and even slept in dragon beds.

Each year in China is ruled over by one of twelve different animals. Recent Years of the Dragon include 1988, 2000, and 2012. According to tradition, a person born in a dragon year will be strong, energetic, popular, and very lucky.

Dragons in Chinese folklore have power over moving bodies of water, such as waterfalls, rivers, and waterspouts. Dragons were important to people living in deserts because they were believed to bring rainfall.

ABOUT THE AUTHOR

Michael Dahl is the author of more than 200 books for children and young adults. He has won the AEP Distinguished Achievement Award three times for his nonfiction. His Finnegan Zwake mystery series was shortlisted twice by the Anthony and Agatha awards. He has also written the *Library of Doom* series. He is a featured speaker at conferences around the country on graphic novels and high-interest books for boys.

GLOSSARY

allies (AL-eyez)—people or countries that give support to each other

astronomer (uh-STRON-uh-mur)—a scientist who studies the stars, planets, and space

birthmark (BURTH-mark)—a mark on the skin that was there from birth

creature (KREE-chur)—a living thing that is human or animal

determination (di-tur-muh-NEY-shuhn)—resolve, or a firm decision to do something

Mongolian (mong-GOH-lee-uhn)—of the area Mongolia. Mongolia is a desert-like country in Asia.

platform (PLAT-form)—a flat, raised structure

rule (ROOL)—have power over something

weapon (WEP-uhn)—something that can be used in a fight to attack or defend

DISCUSSION QUESTIONS

1. When Kong got close to the Hills of the Seven Dragons, his birthmark started to burn. Why did this happen?

2. The stranger on the bus followed the boys. Why do you think he did that? Explain your answer.

3. Kong's grandfather believes in aliens, do you? Why or why not?

WRITING PROMPTS

1. Kong's big adventure included staying in the cave overnight. Write about one of your favorite adventures.

2. Were you surprised by the ending? Write a paragraph describing what you thought would happen at the end.

3. Pick one of the three characters from the story. Then write one more chapter describing what happened to him.

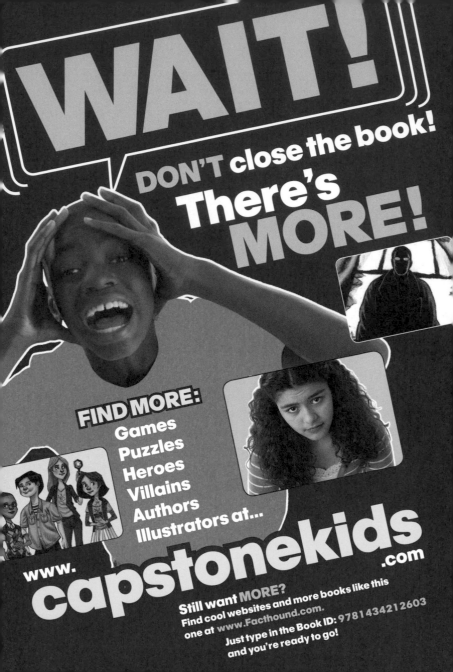

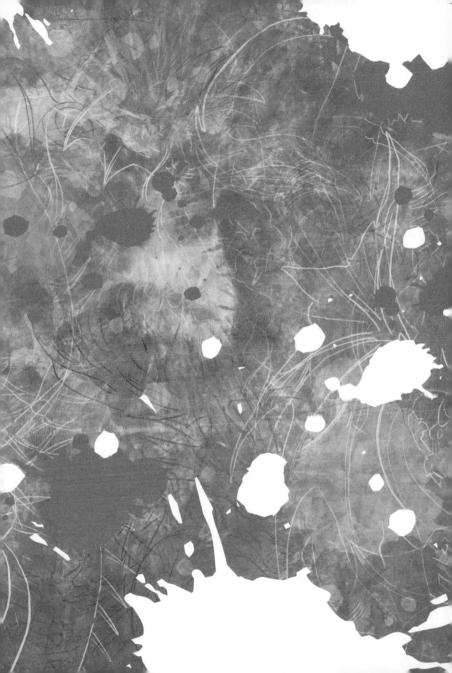

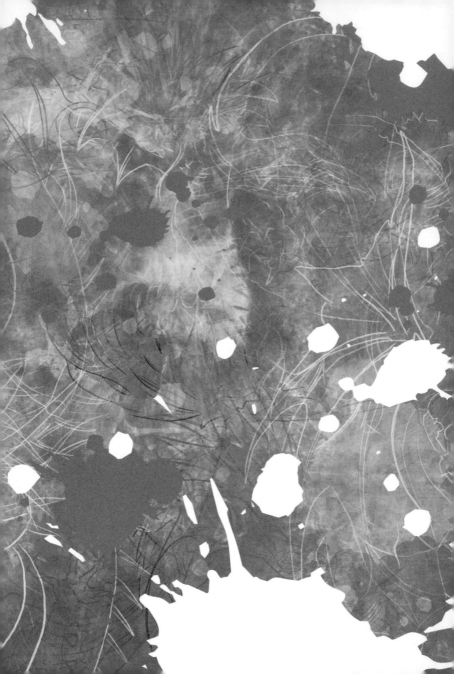

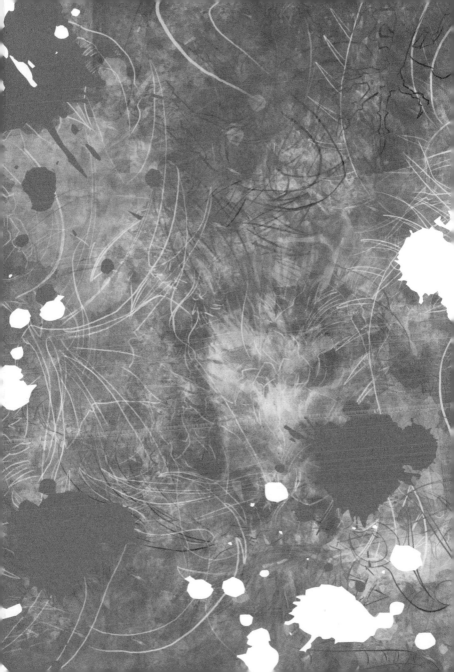

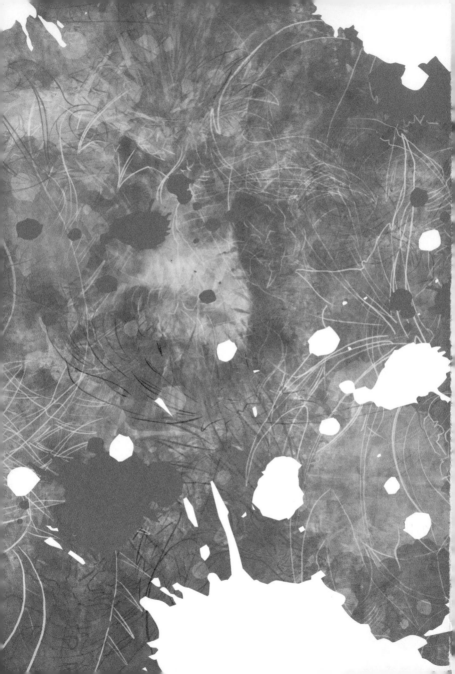